KANGAROOS IN THE KITCHEN?

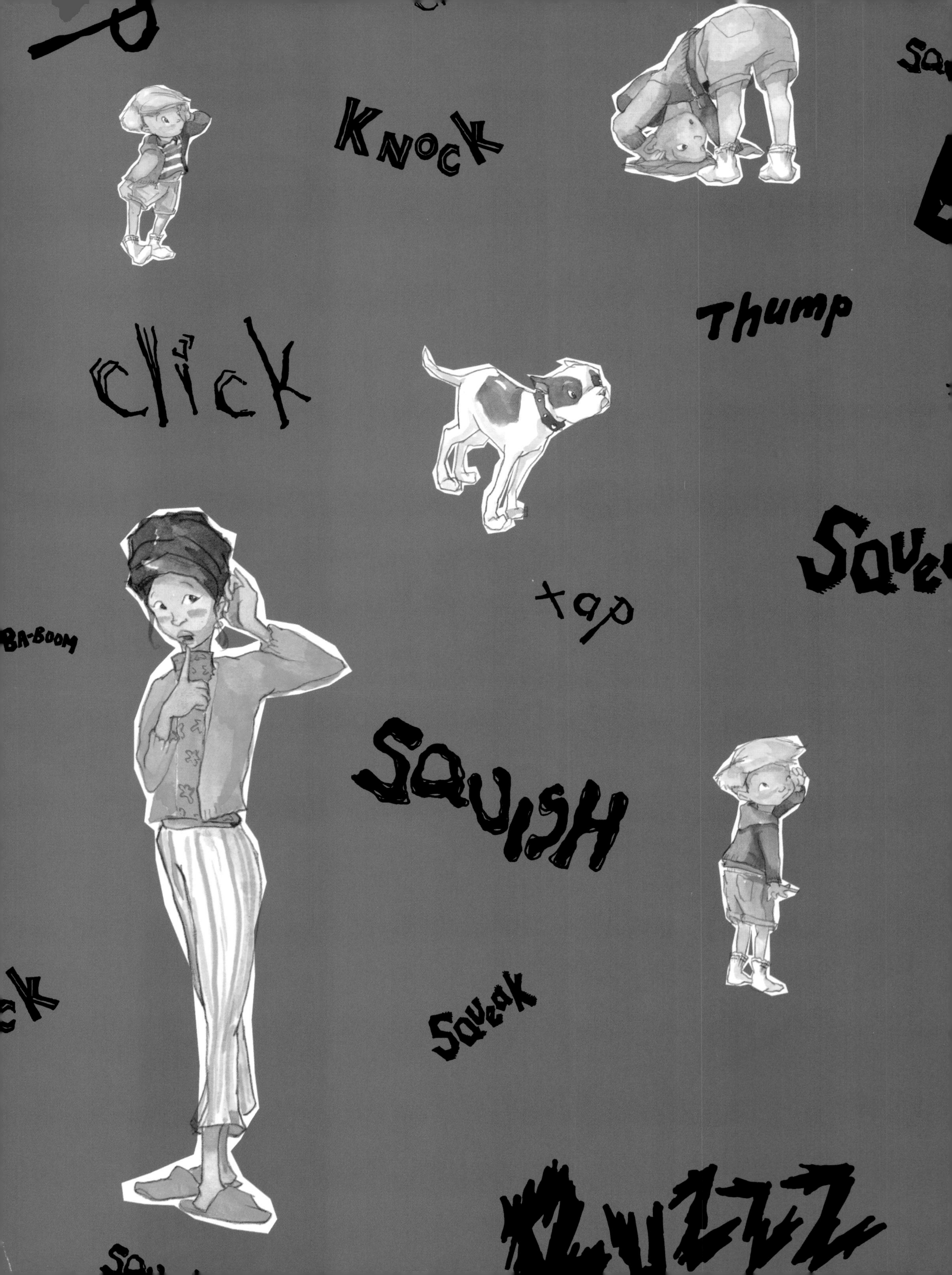

Knock
Thump
click
tap
BA-BOOM
SQUISH
Squeak

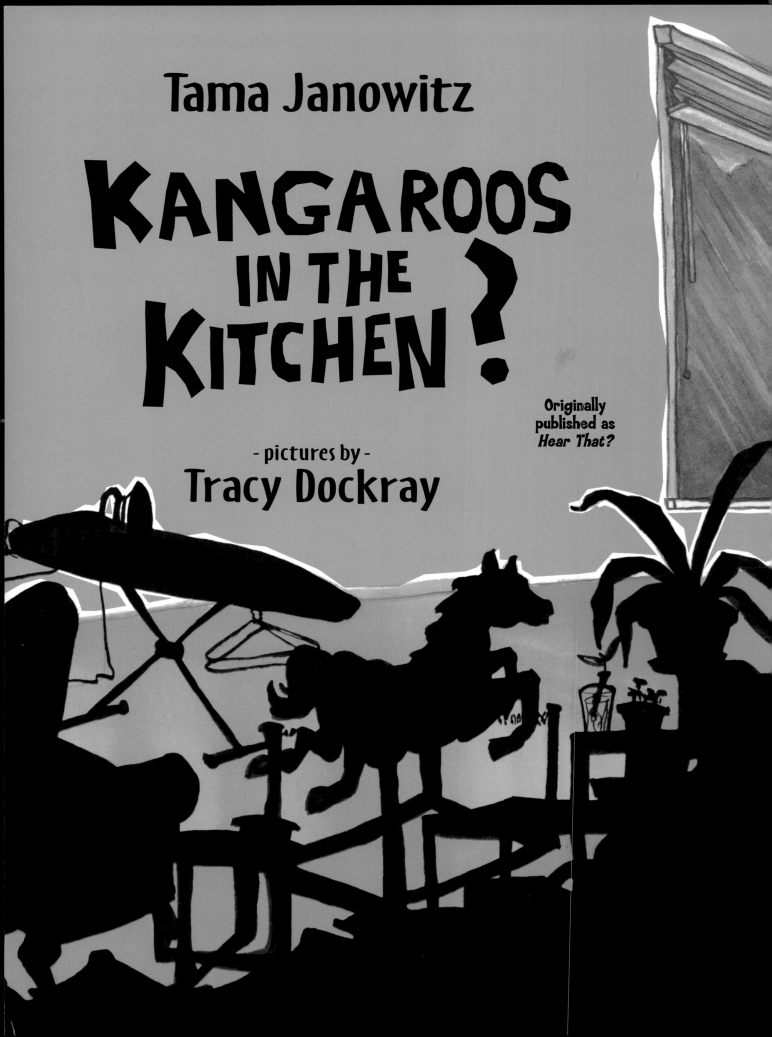

SCHOLASTIC INC.

New York   Toronto   London   Auckland   Sydney
Mexico City   New Delhi   Hong Kong   Buenos Aires

Mom and I were alone at home.

"Ssshhh," I said. "Hear THAT?"

"Yes," said Mom. "Maybe it's Daddy."

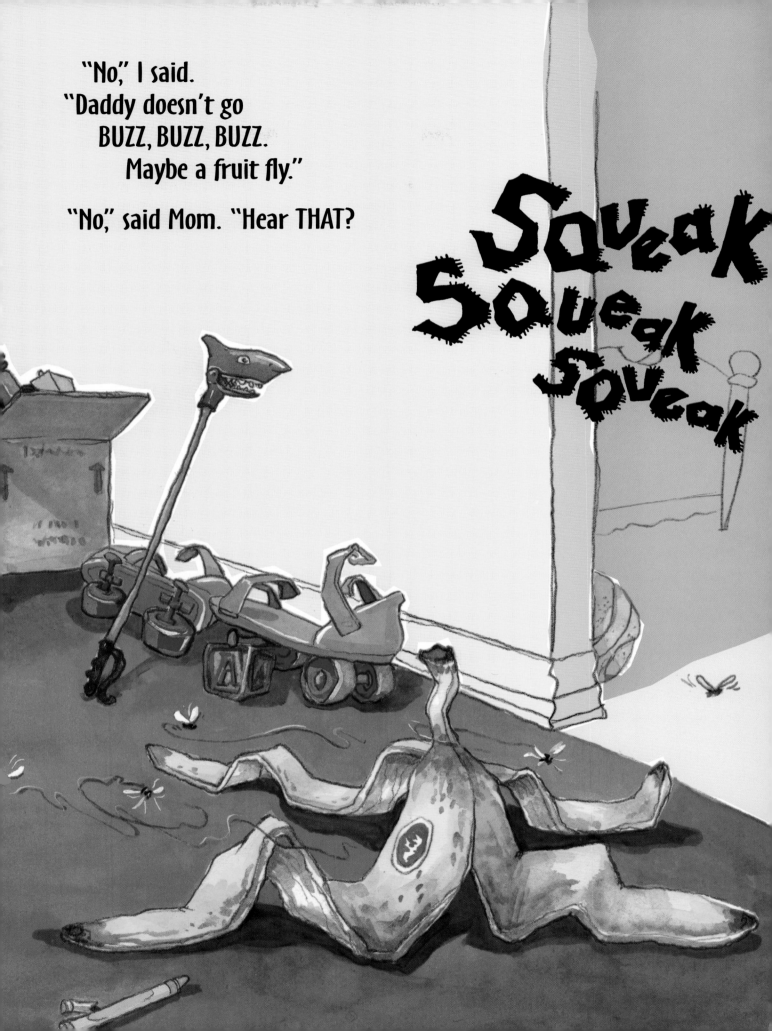

"No," I said.
"Daddy doesn't go
BUZZ, BUZZ, BUZZ.
Maybe a fruit fly."

"No," said Mom. "Hear THAT?

Squeak
Squeak
Squeak

A fly doesn't go
SQUEAK, SQUEAK, SQUEAK."

"Maybe a mouse," I said.
"A mouse munching
on cracker crumbs
under my covers."

"No," said Mom. "Hear THAT?

Mice don't go
    SQUISH, SQUISH, SQUISH."

"Maybe the butler," I said.
"Stepping on that old banana."

"No," said Mom. "Hear THAT?

We don't have a butler
        that goes CLICK, CLICK, CLICK."

    "Maybe sugar ants," I said. "A million sugar ants
                    swarming around the strawberry jelly."

"No," said Mom. "Hear THAT?

tap tap tap tap tap tap tap tap tap tap tap tap tap tap tap tap tap tap

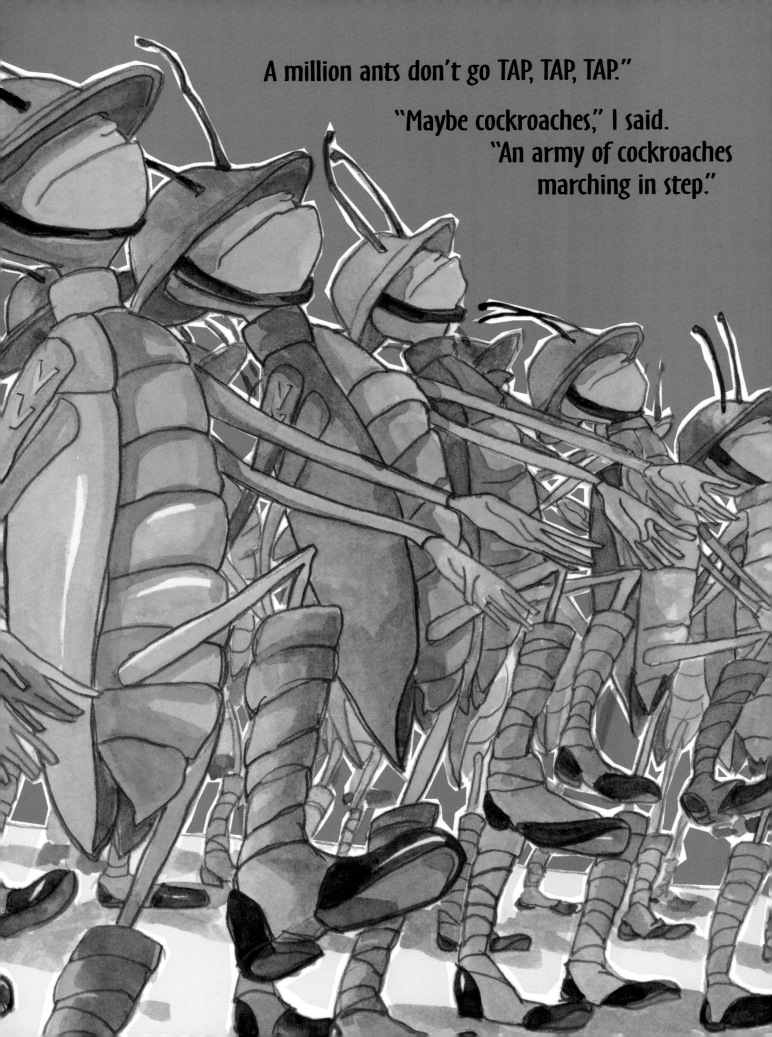

A million ants don't go TAP, TAP, TAP."

"Maybe cockroaches," I said.
"An army of cockroaches marching in step."

"No," said Mom. "Hear THAT?

An army of cockroaches
can't go
KNOCK,
KNOCK,
KNOCK."

"Maybe it's that
old banana," I said.
"Banging on my closet,
where I left his peel."

"No, silly," said Mom.
"Hear THAT?

Bananas don't go THUMP, THUMP, THUMP!"

"Maybe it's our wombat," I said. "Going through the smelly garbage in the kitchen."

"Perhaps," said Mom. "Or even our kangaroos!"

"I know," I said.
"It's the walrus I put in
the refrigerator.

Or even that
     horrible,
     hairy
        ginip-ginop!

Trying to

        escape ...

"No," said Mom.
"Everyone knows
ginip-ginops don't go
BOOM,
BA-BOOM,
BA-BOOM!"

"Maybe we should
go look," I said.
"I'll protect you."

"No ginip-ginops in here," said Mom.
"Or wombats,
        walruses,
               bananas,
                      or butlers."

"It looks like they were," I said.
"They must be hiding."

"Yes," said Mom. "Hear THAT?"

"What else," I said,
    "could go

SQUISH **SQUEAK SQUISH**

Thump **KNOCK** **K**

Buzz **Buzz** **Thump** **KNOC**

Buzz **Thump** tap **BO**

tap

tap

EXCEPT—

"DADDY!"

"I knew it was you, Daddy," I said,
"but Mom was a little scared.

She thought you were
a fruit fly,
and a mouse,
and a butler,
and a million sugar ants,
and an army of cockroaches,
and a banana,
and a wombat,
and a walrus,
and even
a hairy
ginip-ginop!"

"Ssshhh," said Daddy.

"Hear THAT?"

ISBN 0-439-33300-8

Text copyright © 2001 by Tama Janowitz.
Illustrations copyright © 2001 by Tracy Dockray. All rights reserved.
Published by Scholastic Inc., 555 Broadway, New York, NY 10012, by
arrangement with North-South Books, Inc. SCHOLASTIC and associated
logos are trademarks and/or registered trademarks of Scholastic Inc.

12 11 10 9 8 7 6 5 4 3 2 1   2 3 4 5 6 7/0

Printed in the U.S.A.   24

First Scholastic printing, January 2002

The art for this book was prepared using watercolors, Adobe
Illustrator, and Adobe Photoshop. The text for this book
is set in Bitstream Oz Handicraft.

Design by David Andrew DiRienz

For Willow Hunt — T.J.

To Andrea, who creates
order from chaos — T.D.